COWBOY DREAMS

by KATHI APPELT

illustrated by BARRY ROOT

HarperCollins *Publishers*

Cowboy Dreams
Text copyright © 1999 by Kathi Appelt
Illustrations copyright © 1999 by Barrett Root
Printed in the U.S.A. All rights reserved.
http://www.harperchildrens.com

Library of Congress Cataloging-in-Publication Data
Appelt, Kathi, 1954–
    Cowboy dreams / by Kathi Appelt ; pictures by Barry Root.
        p.   cm.
    Summary: A little cowpoke is lulled to sleep by dreams of the sights and sounds of the
Western landscape at night.
    ISBN 0-06-027763-7. — ISBN 0-06-027764-5 (lib. bdg.)
    [1. Cowboys—Fiction.   2. Dreams—Fiction.   3. West (U.S.)—Fiction.   4. Night—
Fiction.   5. Stories in rhyme.]   I. Root, Barry, ill.   II. Title.
PZ8.3.A554Co   1999   98-18316
[E]—dc21   CIP
                                                                                  AC

Typography by Alison Donalty
2   3   4   5   6   7   8   9   10

To my three Williams—
Father, nephew, and the one who led the way
—K.A.

To Kim
—B.R.

Come along, you little cowpoke,

time to turn in for the night.

See the sun slide down the mountain?

See it dip clean out of sight?

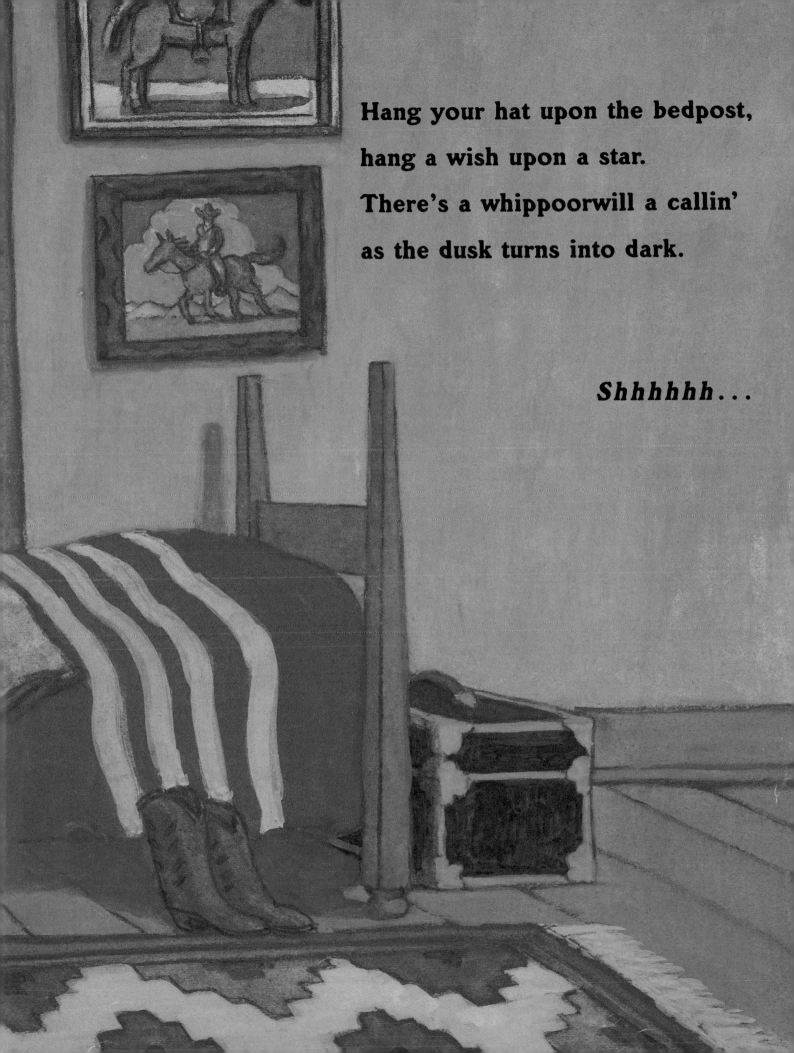

Hang your hat upon the bedpost,
hang a wish upon a star.
There's a whippoorwill a callin'
as the dusk turns into dark.

Shhhhhh...

Can you hear the river murmur
cross the valley deep and green?
Can you hear the night wind whistle
through the river's bedside trees?

The prairie fox is stirring,
the owl is on the wing,
La Luna's in her nightgown
with its matching silver ring.

She'll keep her lantern glowing
as she slips across the sky.
Camp Cookie tips his hat
and joins the evening lullaby.

Yippee ti-yi-yo, little dogies,
that's the song the cowboys croon.
Above, the star-bears blink their eyes
to hear that sleepy tune.

His sturdy legs have carried you
across so many miles.
No other pony can compare.
La Luna watches, smiles.

Your palomino hears the song.
He shakes his silky head.
La Luna dusts his golden coat
with sparkling silver thread.

The stars in soft-warm silver
dance above coyote's lair.
You can see the nighthawk's shadow
as she lifts into the air.

She glides upon the evening breeze
that brushes through her wings.
"Sleep tight, sleep tight, compadre,"
the little night bird sings.

Below, cicadas chirrup,
"Go to sleep, my saddle pal."
while La Luna casts her lantern light
across the chaparral.

She'll keep the night watch comp'ny
as the evening rolls on by.
Camp Cookie tips his hat again
and ends his lullaby.

So, lay your head down on your saddle,
pull your bedroll 'neath your chin.
Softly, softly lowing cattle
settle down as night rolls in.

Close your eyes now, li'l pardner,
lasso up those cowboy dreams.
La Luna's warmed your blanket
in her satin silver beams.

She's set coyote callin',
"Yip yip yaroo . . . yip yip yaroo!"
Good night, good night, my darlin',
happy trails, my buckaroo!